For the original Kit, Josie and Amy
with love from Dad

STAR QUEST
VOYAGE TO THE GREYLON GALAXY

Join Captain Kit Johnson and his crew for a thrilling space adventure in the alien Greylon Galaxy!

Alan Durant wrote *Star Quest: Voyage to the Greylon Galaxy* in response to his son Kit's desire for "fast-paced Star Wars/Star Trek type adventure. There's lots of jokey space stories for junior school children, but very little straight sci-fi adventure." In this book, for the first time, Alan's given characters the names of all three of his children – Kit, Amy and Josie. Look out for more Star Quest adventures coming your way soon!

Alan's other books for children include two about *Spider McDrew* and *Little Troll*, three about Creepe Hall and eight in the Leggs United series about a family football team managed by a ghost! Among his books for older children are the thrillers *Blood* and *Publish or Die*, and *The Kingfisher Book of Vampire and Werewolf Stories*, which he compiled. Alan lives in a fairly ordinary house just south of London with his wife, three children, cat and a garden shed in which he does all his writing.

Books by the same author

Creepe Hall
Return to Creepe Hall
Creepe Hall For Ever!
Jake's Magic
Spider McDrew
Happy Birthday, Spider McDrew
Little Troll
Leggs United (series)
The Fantastic Football Fun Book

STAR QUEST

VOYAGE TO THE GREYLON GALAXY

ALAN DURANT

Illustrations by

MICK BROWNFIELD

WALKER BOOKS

AND SUBSIDIARIES

LONDON • BOSTON • SYDNEY

J81,820
£3·99

First published 1999 by Walker Books Ltd
87 Vauxhall Walk, London SE11 5HJ

This edition published 2000

10 9 8 7 6 5 4 3 2 1

This book has been typeset in Plantin.

Printed in England by Clays Ltd, St Ives plc

British Library Cataloguing in Publication Data
A catalogue record for this book
is available from the British Library.

ISBN 0-7445-6977-X

CONTENTS

CALLING KIT JOHNSON!

Kit Johnson was sitting in the Star Quest Academy dining hall when the call came. He was about to take a bite of his high protein root burger when a loud beeping drew his attention to the huge video screen. The Commander's face appeared. He looked very serious.

"Cadet Kit Johnson to the operations area at once," the Commander ordered. "This is an emergency!" Then the Commander's face faded and the screen went dark once more.

A murmur of excitement went round the dining hall. Kit could sense people staring at him as he put down his burger and stood up. Hands shaking a little, he picked up his red cap and walked to the door. What on earth could the Commander want of him? he wondered nervously. Had he done something wrong?

If so, he couldn't think what. He was always near the top of his class in the Academy and several of the instructors had said that they expected him to become a Star Quest Adventurer one day like his dad, Dr Marcus Johnson.

Dr Marcus Johnson was a legend at the Academy: he was one of the greatest Adventurers ever. His voyages to the Greylon Galaxy and beyond had made him a world hero. But in the end they had cost him dear, for he had not returned from his last voyage. No one knew what had happened to him. Along with his Questship *Icarus 1* and all of its crew, he had simply vanished in space.

An Adventurer's life was full of risks and dangers and few lived to an old age. Still, Dr Marcus's disappearance had come as a terrible shock to Kit and to his mother, who was an instructor at the Academy, and to his little sister, Josie, who was in the class below him. Kit still hoped that one day his father would return, but after two years that hope was little more than a glimmer.

Kit had been nine when his father had disappeared. He'd been born during the war with the Zedek Empire. On the day of his birth, the Earth had suffered a particularly fierce radiation attack that had killed many people. Kit had only survived because of the magical healing crystals his father had recently brought back from the Greylon Galaxy. The combined effect of the radiation and the crystals had left Kit with a super power: at the age of eleven he was stronger than most men.

There was something else unusual about Kit – his eyes. The right one was brown and the left one was blue. The brown one was real, but the blue one was a cybereye. It had been put in by his father to replace the real left eye, which had been destroyed in the Zedek attack. The cybereye looked like a normal eye but it was ten times more powerful. Through it, Kit could see far into the distance ahead and on either side of him.

Right now, both eyes were focussing on the door to the operations area, at the heart of which was the Commander's office. He hesitated a moment, then punched in his number: KJ15791. The buttons beeped as he pushed them and then hummed as his number was accepted. A green light flashed and a robotic voice spoke. "Cadet Kit Johnson, you may enter the operations area. Please step forward now." The door slid aside and with a small pulse of excitement Kit walked through.

He had never been in the operations area before. This was the brain of the Academy. It was here that missions were planned and important decisions taken. Kit looked around him, his cybereye quickly taking in the whole area. On all sides men and women sat with headphones, before computer screens, while other larger computers clicked and whirred and, now and then, a light flashed red or white or green. Large video screens showed other parts of the Academy. Glancing up at one, Kit could see the dining hall he had just left, where some of his classmates were still eating.

"Fascinating, eh?" said a voice beside him. Kit flinched and turned quickly. A tall man in a Star Quest officer's uniform was smiling at him. He had very blue eyes. Kit raised his hand in a salute. "Cadet Kit Johnson, I presume," said the officer.

"Yes, sir," Kit nodded, his fair hair flopping on to his forehead.

The officer put his hand to his Star Quest emblem. "Colonel Alexander," he said warmly. "I knew your father well. I was with him on several of his voyages."

"Yes, sir." Kit knew of Colonel Alexander. His father had mentioned him many times. He was also a hero, as the zigzag strip of gold on his uniform proved. The Gold Lightning Flash was the Academy's highest badge of bravery.

"If you'll follow me, I'll take you to the Commander's office," said Colonel

Alexander. Then he raised his thick eyebrows. "He's impatient to see you."

PHASE 2

STAR QUEST CAPTAIN

The Commander was speaking into his videophone when Colonel Alexander and Kit entered his office. He waved at them to sit down.

"I want to know as soon as there are any developments," he growled into the phone. "Any developments at all. Is that clear?"

"Sir!" a voice cried crisply in reply.

"Good," said the Commander. He pressed a button and the videophone shut down. When he looked up, his face was grim and as grey as his hair.

"We have a serious problem," he said gravely. "And very little time to sort it out. So I want you to listen very carefully to what I'm going to tell you, Kit. Understand?"

Kit frowned. "Yes, sir," he said with a puzzled air. What important thing could the

Commander have to tell *him*, a simple cadet? It was all very strange.

"For some years, as you will be aware, relations between Earth and the Greylon Galaxy have been severely strained," the Commander continued. "Your father brought back minerals, healing crystals, that saved our world, but in taking them he upset the Greylons, who accused us of intergalactic robbery. They threatened to make war. We only managed to avoid this by giving the Greylons some of our precious minerals in return.

"Now a new crisis has arisen. This morning we received a message from the Greylons informing us that an Earthship had entered their Galaxy and stolen some of their healing crystals. There was a fight and one of the Earthship's crew was captured. The others and the ship itself escaped. The Greylons are demanding that these thieves be caught and punished and the crystals returned. If this is not done within two star days, the Greylon Galaxy will declare war on Earth."

The Commander looked hard into Kit's face, his eyes full of determination. "This must not happen," he said firmly. "A war against the Greylon Galaxy would be a disaster. It would mean an end to the supply of healing crystals that are vital to our world. Besides, our forces are already fully stretched defending this planet from Zedek attacks. Do you understand?"

Kit nodded. "Yes, sir," he said. But he was still puzzled – what did all of this have to do with *him*?

His unspoken question was soon answered.

"You will be wondering why I have called you here," said the Commander. "Am I right?"

"Yes, sir," Kit said.

A hint of a smile appeared on the Commander's face. Then he nodded and pursed his lips. "We are in a difficult situation," he said. "Our Questships are all out on patrol and none is close enough to the Greylon Galaxy to meet the deadline the

Greylon Command has set us. Only a ship travelling direct from Earth could do that."

"But you have no ships, sir," Kit objected.

"No regular Questships, no," said the Commander. "But we do have a ship."

Kit frowned as he realized what the Commander meant.

"The XL?" he said. "But that's just a training craft."

The XL was the small spaceship on which the Academy cadets practised their Star Quest skills.

"Beggars can't be choosers," Colonel Alexander observed dryly.

"At this very moment," the Commander went on, "the XL is being transformed into a fully operational Questship, albeit a small one."

"I see," said Kit. But he didn't really. It was all very bemusing.

"All it needs now is a crew," said Colonel Alexander and both he and the Commander stared at Kit.

Now, at last, Kit understood!

"You want me to be part of a Star Quest crew?" he said. "Is that it? But I'm only a cadet."

The Commander smiled more openly now. "You are an Academy cadet," he said. "Every pupil who attends this Academy has been hand-picked for their outstanding qualities, abilities, skills and intelligence. But even among them you, Kit, are exceptional – as too are a few of your fellow students. With the training you have had, we are confident you are more than ready for action. In fact we believe that you are the best man for this job."

"Wow!" Kit uttered. He was amazed but, at the same time, totally thrilled. "Me, part of a Questship crew." He never imagined in his wildest dreams that his ambition would be fulfilled so soon. But there was a yet greater surprise to come.

"We want you to be more than part of the crew," the Commander continued. "We want

you to be captain of a special cadet team.
From this moment you are Star Quest
Captain Kit Johnson."

J9, 820

MEETING THE CREW

....

After a two-hour briefing from the
Commander and Colonel Alexander, Captain
Kit Johnson finally stood before his
spaceship. He studied it carefully. The ship
was small, no bigger than a spaceshuttle
really, but well-equipped. Its computer
technology was as advanced as the best
Questship's, Colonel Alexander said, and
though its laser weaponry and defence shields
were less powerful, they were still excellent
for a craft of its size. It was fast too, having
just been fitted with new engines, and able to
turn very quickly – a useful advantage in
battle.

"We've given it a new name too," said
Colonel Alexander. "A proper name." He
took Kit to the front of the ship and pointed
to the platinum nameplate.

24

"*Icarus 2*," Kit read and a lump rose in his throat. "It's a good name," he said.

"Perhaps one day *Icarus 2* will fly alongside *Icarus 1*," said Colonel Alexander, and he put his hand on Kit's shoulder.

"Your father could still be out there somewhere, Kit – you know, alive. This person the Greylons are holding…" He let the suggestion hang in the air, his eyebrows raised.

"Dad?" Kit queried. "You think it might be Dad? But—"

"I don't know, Kit," said Colonel Alexander. "But the *Icarus 1* vanished on a mission to the Greylon Galaxy and suddenly this unidentified Earthship appears from nowhere… All I'm saying is that there may be more to this than meets the eye." The Colonel's blue eyes held Kit's in a piercing stare. Kit would have liked to question his superior officer further, but they were already at the entrance to the ship.

"Now, come and meet your crew," Colonel Alexander said.

The crew was a small one – just four members. Two of them were waiting for Kit as he stepped through the door of the loading dock. The first to catch his eye was a slight, dark-skinned boy with a creamy half-moon on his forehead. Kit nodded at him and smiled.

"Hi, Sunny," he said warmly. "I hoped you'd be coming."

The boy smiled back. "It is an honour," he said.

"Dr Sunil Patel will be your Science and Medical officer," said Colonel Alexander.

Sunil Patel was the first child from the moon colony, Lunax, to attend the Star Quest Academy. Like Kit, just eleven years old, he was a double doctor – of medicine and engineering. He was always very neat and had a very calm, grown-up manner. He didn't say a lot but what he did say was usually worth listening to. Kit and he had been friends since they started at the Academy. His feelings for the boy standing next to Sunny, however, were not so warm. He eyed him now warily: a tall, burly boy with a pale freckly face, flame red hair and sparky blue eyes.

"Hello, Red," Kit said.

"Good day, Captain," replied the burly boy curtly.

"Lieutenant Stravinsky – Red – will be your navigator and second-in-command," said Colonel Alexander. He looked from one boy to the other. "I'm sure you'll work together very well. The future of Star Quest could be in your hands."

"Of course," said Kit, and the other boy nodded. But neither looked particularly happy.

Kit and Red had long been rivals. Red had his gang of friends and Kit his and they were usually on opposing sides in any fight or argument. Red was a little jealous of Kit and his famous father and Kit considered Red to be over-aggressive and rude. Finding out that they were to be fellow crew members did not fill Kit with pleasure.

His spirits were lifted considerably, however, on reaching the control room and discovering the third member of the crew. She was studying a computer console, but looked up and grinned when the others entered the room.

"Hi, skipper," she said with a mock salute.

"Hi, sis," Kit replied, grinning back.

"Your sister, Josie, will take care of all computer operations on the voyage," said Colonel Alexander.

"You bet yer," Josie declared, spinning round again to face her console.

Kit stared at his little sister. From behind, with her slender build and short blonde hair, she looked like a boy. She often acted like a boy too, which got her into trouble sometimes, because she wasn't as tough as she thought she was. Kit was pleased she'd been chosen to come on this mission – she could work computers better than anyone he knew – but he'd have to look out for her. He wondered briefly what his mother would say about the two of them going off on such a major quest – especially as it was to the Greylon Galaxy, where their father had disappeared. She'd be concerned, he was sure of that, but she'd be proud too. This was a mission that had to be undertaken.

"And now," said Colonel Alexander, "let me introduce you to the final member of your crew. Meet I-See." He gestured towards the other side of the room. Peering over, Kit saw a stocky, child-sized blue robot with a pleasant expression.

A short antenna rose from his head and most of his body was taken up with a large oval computer monitor, which at this moment was showing an image of a huge smiley face.

"I-See is an independent computeroid," Colonel Alexander continued. "He has the most advanced program in existence. He's almost as human as you or I. You'll find him an invaluable aid in communicating with the Greylons, as he can speak and understand every known language. He even flashes the translation up on his screen. Isn't that so, I-See?"

"Ixplaco-oh," I-See warbled cheerfully and the word "yes" appeared clearly on his monitor.

"A most interesting language," he remarked.

"Sounds crazy to me," said Red.

"No doubt our language sounds equally bizarre to the inhabitants of Greylon," I-See stated.

"Well, we'll find out soon enough," said Kit with calm determination. He looked about his new ship with pride: the high-tec computer consoles, the powerful monitors, the brand-new, ergonomically advanced furnishing, the gleaming metallic walls – everything superbly designed and crafted for maximum comfort and effectiveness. There was no doubt about it – the *Icarus 2* was a state-of-the-art Questship.

"You're quite right," said Colonel

Alexander. "There's not a moment to lose. You must set off at once." He raised his hand in a Star Quest salute, which each of the *Icarus* crew members returned – even I-See, who clinked his metal fingers together. Then Colonel Alexander turned and strode towards the door. He stopped just before it and looked round, his Gold Lightning Flash glinting in the artificial light.

"The best of luck, all of you," he said. "The Commander expects great things of you – and so do I. The fate of this planet could well be in your hands. Don't let us down."

"We won't, sir," Kit promised. "You can count on us." He watched the Colonel's form disappear through the doorway, then moved to take the skipper's seat for the first time.

"Right, everyone!" he called. "Action stations. Red, set a course for the Greylon Galaxy. Sunny, fire up the engines. Josie, run a final computer check. I-See, start the countdown." A throb of power vibrated through the ship as the engines started.

"This is it, everyone," Kit cried. "Belts on! Prepare for take off!"

PHASE 4

FIRST CONTACT

Hurtling through space at a speed of over one thousand galactic knots, the *Icarus 2* was soon in sight of Galileo 2, the large star that marked the edge of the galaxy. Beyond lay Middle Space, the empty area that separated Earth and its universe from the Greylon Galaxy.

Unstrapped and at ease in the comfortable skipper's chair, Captain Kit Johnson was trying in vain to keep his mind focused on the quest before him. So much had happened in the last few hours. There was so much to think about. His dad, for a start. Kit knew he couldn't be a space pirate. But he might have been captured by them. If so, then he might have let himself be taken by the Greylons on purpose to escape from the pirates. That's just the sort of thing his dad would do, Kit thought. In fact the more he thought about it, the surer he became that this was the truth. He started to believe that the prisoner held by the Greylons was his dad and a wave of excited anticipation rushed through him. He couldn't wait for them to get to their destination.

Red's voice brought Kit back to the present. "Entering Middle Space," he announced.

"The scanner indicates a possible meteor storm," said Josie, staring into one of the monitors before her.

"Is that anything to worry about, Sunny?" Kit asked.

Sunny examined his own console. "It appears to be merely a small shower," he declared. "We should be through with but minor inconvenience."

"An entirely accurate assessment," I-See agreed and a large red tick filled his monitor.

Sunny was right. They saw the meteors on the screen but barely felt their impact. It was like someone had pelted the ship with crab-apples.

"Thank goodness for that," said Kit as the blackness of Middle Space slipped by. "Now we can head full speed to Greylon."

No sooner had he spoken than there was a yelp from Red.

"Vessel approaching on the starboard side!" he cried. "A thousand galactic metres and closing fast."

"Any identification?" Kit demanded.

"No formal identification, but it looks like an Earthship," said Red, his pale face whiter than ever.

"An Earthship out here?" queried Kit. "Are you sure?"

Red glanced at Kit with a spark of anger.

"It's an Earthship," he hissed. "Look up at the control screen if you don't believe me."

Kit looked up. The control screen showed a big grey ship whizzing straight at them: on collision course! Kit struggled to remain calm.

"Can we make contact, Josie?" he asked.

Josie flicked buttons on her console. There were several beeps and whirrs. "Negative, Captain," she said, shaking her head. "Their computers do not respond."

"They're almost on us, for goodness' sake!" Red shouted, his voice cracking with tension.

"Move into evasive orbit, Red," Kit commanded. "Go!"

There was no time even to strap up. In an instant, the *Icarus 2* swerved sharply with a violence that sent Kit and Sunny tumbling from their seats. Kit reached out for something to break his fall, but as the ship jolted again, he crashed heavily to the floor.

It seemed, for a few seconds, as if the craft would veer dangerously out of control. Kit looked up at the control screen, fearing the worst, but gradually the *Icarus 2* straightened up and stabilized. Red had the ship back on line. The collision had been avoided – fortunately for the *Icarus*. Another second's delay and the small Questship would have been smashed to pieces, its crew dropping helplessly through space…

Red waved his hand angrily.

"Crazy idiots!" he cried. "They'd have hit us if we hadn't moved."

"I rather imagine that was their plan," said Sunny, dusting himself down with great care.

"But why would they want to ram us?" Kit said, perplexed.

"Maybe they wanted to give us a scare," Josie suggested.

"They did that all right!" exclaimed Red. He turned to Kit. "You didn't give me much time to get clear."

Kit glared back. "They didn't give us much time, did they?" he said. He took a deep breath. "Any more on who they might be, sis?" he asked.

"I have some pictures taken by our photo-sensors as the ship passed," Josie said. "But I don't know how clear they'll be."

"Run them anyway," Kit directed and he looked up once more at the vast control screen.

Images appeared of the Earthship with which they had so nearly collided.

"Freeze that one!" Kit cried at a picture of the craft's bow. "Now, enlarge to the maximum, please." Josie pressed a button at her right-hand side and the picture zoomed out at them. "Look, there!" Kit said.

"A skull and crossbones," Red breathed.

"Space pirates," Sunny stated calmly. "And heading out of the Greylon Galaxy."

"Yes," said Kit. "I think we may have found our crystal thieves." Then with a grim face he added, "And lost them." He stared at the dark screen, in which only a few distant, twinkling stars were visible. They were on the borders of the Greylon Galaxy. Once more Kit felt a surge of excitement as he realized they were about to enter alien territory for the first time in their lives.

"We'd better make a communication link-up with the Greylons to tell them we're coming," he said. "We don't want them to think we're pirates and attack us. I-See, I think this is a job for you. Josie will assist you."

"Ixplaco-oh, Captain," I-See said cheerily, the word "yes" flashing up on his screen.

As the robot crossed the room, Kit turned to Red with a steely look. "Full speed ahead to the Greylon Galaxy, Lieutenant Stravinsky," he ordered.

IN THE GREYLON GALAXY

....

The Greylons were far from welcoming to their human visitors.

They guided *Icarus 2* to a landing-place on their planet, but refused to allow anyone to leave the ship. Instead, a party of Greylons boarded *Icarus 2*. They stood now in the control room, facing Kit and his crew.

Kit gazed at the Greylons in fascination. He had seen holograms of Greylons, but he had never seen one in the flesh before. They were tall and greeny-grey with eagle-like heads and beaks, and had sharp talons instead of fingers and toes. They had no hair, but a stiff fan of skin that stood up on their heads. The one in front, who seemed to be their leader, wore a purple cloak. He opened his beak and spoke strange, fierce sounds. Kit looked at I-See's monitor for a translation.

"My name is Sark and I am Overlord of the Greylon Galaxy," he read.

Kit nodded. "Tell him who we are and that we have come in answer to their call," Kit said. He listened as I-See uttered a stream of hard sounds that were quickly returned by the Greylon Lord. Kit read the reply: "I am greatly surprised and troubled by the youth of this Star Quest crew. I fear that Earth does not appreciate the gravity of the situation."

Kit gave the Greylon Lord a proud look. "Tell his Lordship that we may be young but we are fully trained and equipped for duty. He should not underestimate us. Assure him that Earth takes his threats very seriously. That is why we have come so quickly."

I-See uttered another torrent of harsh sounds at which the Greylon Lord nodded and spoke again.

"Your words are good," he said. "I hope your actions match them." The two leaders stood for a moment, eyeball to eyeball, as if each was searching for any sign of weakness in the other. Then Kit instructed I-See to ask Sark for permission to see the Earth prisoner. Sark replied that he would allow Kit and I-See alone to enter the Greylons' palace, where the prisoner was being held.

"Very well," said Kit. He turned to Red. "You're in charge of the ship, Red, while I'm gone. Josie, make sure all communication channels are left open."

Josie nodded and frowned. "Be careful, skip," she said.

"Don't worry about me, sis," Kit replied lightly. "I'll be OK." Then he grinned. "I've got I-See to look after me."

"I shall do my best, Captain," I-See burbled and on to his monitor leapt a roaring lion.

Josie smiled briefly, but her face was unusually anxious. She watched as Kit and I-See joined the Greylons. The Greylon Lord growled a command and, a heartbeat later, the whole group dematerialized, vanishing completely.

*   *   *

Kit found himself in an enormous indoor complex. He peered around, his cybereye focusing on every detail. There were no windows and the high roof was round and silver. In the centre of the room, raised off the floor on a high platform, was a kind of capsule. It too was silver and metallic. It was towards this that his Greylon hosts now led him. As they approached it, Kit could feel his pulse start to race and his heart beat faster. He wasn't thinking with the calm head of a Star Quest Captain, but then at this particular instant he didn't feel like a Star Quest Captain; he felt like an eleven-year-old boy desperate to see his dad.

They climbed an escalator to the raised platform. The door to the capsule opened and Sark motioned Kit to enter. Then he pointed at I-See and barked an order. Kit alone could enter.

"It appears I must remain here," said I-See. Kit nodded.

He moved to enter the capsule, but as he

did so the Greylon Lord reached out one taloned hand and held his shoulder, speaking as he did so.

"He wants you to know that they'll be watching," I-See translated. "There's a surveillance monitor inside."

Kit shrugged away Sark's hand. "Tell him I am glad," he said. "We have nothing to hide."

Then, as I-See delivered this message, Kit stepped forward eagerly into the capsule.

PHASE 6

AMY ADAIR

....

Inside the capsule was a single bare room, brightly lit. At the centre of the roof a surveillance globe hovered. At the edge of the light, in one corner, a figure sat, head down, knees hunched, wrapped in a dark cloak. Kit stepped forward tentatively.

"Dad?" he inquired uncertainly.

For a second or two there was no reaction. Then, slowly, the figure stirred, raised its head.

"Oh!" Kit cried with a mixture of surprise and disappointment. The prisoner was not Dr Marcus Johnson; she was a young girl, probably no older than himself. Olive-skinned with black bobbed hair, she glared at him through large moon-round green eyes, framed by long, spidery lashes. She wore old sandals on her feet and beneath the opened cloak her clothes, Kit could see, were ragged and torn. Kit's mum would have said the girl looked as if she could do with a good meal and a good scrub.

The girl eyed Kit suspiciously. "Who are you?" she demanded in a low, fierce voice. Kit returned her look with a hard-eyed stare, trying to regain his composure.

"I am Captain Kit Johnson of the Questship *Icarus 2* and I have been sent to arrest you and your fellow pirates and recover the crystals you have stolen."

"Huh," uttered the girl with a proud shrug of her head. "You're only a boy."

"I am a Star Quest Captain," he replied proudly. "Who are you?"

"What's it to you?" said the girl rudely, pulling her cloak tightly about her once more.

"If you tell me, I might be able to help you," Kit said. "No one else here will."

"You don't want to help me," said the girl, "you just want to take me back to Earth and put me in prison." She drew up her knees and bowed her head, hiding her face behind her dark arms, on each of which, Kit noticed now, she wore a thick, gold bracelet. At the centre of the bracelets was a striking purple stone that Kit had never seen before.

Staring at the hunched-up figure before him, Kit couldn't help feeling sorry for the girl, despite her unfriendly manner. He imagined how unhappy he would feel if he were all alone, imprisoned on an alien planet. He went over and knelt down beside her. He held out his arm and touched her gently on the shoulder. She flinched.

"I don't want to lock you away," he said. "I just want to sort things out. But I need your help. I need to know what's been going on."

"You want me to betray my ship, is that it?" the girl muttered from behind her arms.

"No," said Kit. "I want you to help me stop a war that will cause misery and death and perhaps destroy two planets. No spaceship can be worth the risk of a war like that."

For a few moments, the two remained

completely motionless and silent. Then the girl lifted her head and looked at Kit.

"I'm not a pirate," she said simply. "My name's Amy Adair and I'm from the Earth colony Spartacus 9. The pirates raided us a year ago and they took me prisoner. There was no way of escape so I had to do what they said. I had to become one of them."

"But who are they?" Kit asked.

"They come from the prison colony Oberon. There was a revolt there and they broke out and stole a spaceship. They've been roaming different galaxies since, robbing other ships and planets. They came to Greylon to steal the healing crystals. Silver found out how valuable they were to people on Earth. He thought he could sell them for a high price."

"Is Silver their leader?" Kit asked.

Amy nodded.

"It's a strange name," Kit said thoughtfully.

Amy tossed her head. "Ha!" she cried. "That's just what he calls himself. He got the name from some old story. I don't know what his real name is."

"How many pirates are there on the ship?" Kit asked.

"Ten," Amy replied. Then she frowned, sighed. "No, nine, now."

The two sat side by side without speaking for a while, then Kit produced a small hologram from a mechanism in his belt. He showed it to Amy. "Is this man among the pirates?" he asked softly.

Amy shook her head. "Who is he?" she said.

"He's my father, Captain Marcus Johnson," Kit replied, staring wistfully at the hologram.

Amy's green eyes flickered. "I've heard of him," she said. "Silver hates him. I think they had a fight once and Silver lost."

"When was this, do you know?" Kit demanded eagerly, hope once more kicking inside him.

Amy shrugged. "I'm sorry, I don't," she murmured apologetically. "It was before the pirates took me."

Kit nodded and sighed. It was even more vital now that he find those pirates. He shut down the hologram, then looked straight into Amy's green eyes. "I'm going to need your help, Amy," he said firmly, "to catch these pirates."

"And if you do, what happens then?" Amy said.

"We'll return the crystals to the Greylons and take Silver and his crew back to Earth for trial," said Kit.

"What about me?" Amy asked.

"You'll come back with us," said Kit.

Amy bowed her head again. "To prison," she murmured glumly.

Kit turned to face her. "No, not if you help us," he said. "I'll speak up for you, I promise." He put his hand on her arm, above the bracelet. Slowly, she raised her head until she was looking him in the eyes.

"If you get me out of here," she said, "I'll help you."

"Great," Kit said with a smile. Then he

stood up. "I wish to leave!" he called, staring into the surveillance globe and gesturing towards the door. There was a beep and a shushing sound as the door started to open. Kit pulled Amy to her feet. "Stay close to me," he hissed. Then he moved quickly across the room and through the doorway to where I-See stood, waiting for him.

"I am happy to see you, Captain," I-See warbled, a grinning face appearing on his monitor. The grin became a frown. "But I fear we have a problem."

Kit looked ahead and saw a couple of Greylon guards appearing at the top of the escalator, weapons ready, moving menacingly towards them. Kit stepped forward purposefully. The guards raised their weapons.

"Tell them to let us pass," Kit instructed I-See. I-See approached the guards and spoke to them in their language. One of them shook his head and waved his weapon.

"I'm afraid they refuse," I-See reported.

"Then we'll have to leave without their

permission," said Kit grimly. "Send a message to the *Icarus*, I-See. Give them our exact position and tell them to prepare to take us and our prisoner on board without delay."

I-See followed his captain's orders. But while he was still completing his communication with the *Icarus*, the Greylon guards suddenly sprang forward to take hold of Amy. It was time for Kit to use his special strength. Surprised, but quick to react, he struck out at the first guard and knocked him aside. Then he leapt at the second guard, who already had one talon on Amy's arm. The guard let go of Amy and fought with Kit instead. The young Star Quest Captain was strong, but so too was the Greylon guard. Locked in struggle, the two figures dropped to the ground.

A harsh angry voice suddenly grated the air. At once, the Greylon guard released his hold on Kit and rolled away. Kit looked up, panting. Sark was standing over him, his face more hostile than ever. Behind him was a large group of guards.

The Greylon Lord rasped another string of sounds, pointing a talon accusingly at Kit. The message was clear. He wanted to know what on earth Kit was doing. Kit got up slowly. He dusted himself down.

"Tell the Lord Sark what happened, I-See. Tell him that we demand – no, request – to be allowed to leave with our prisoner."

I-See's words did not go down well. Sark spat out a furious reply that Kit had no right to take the Greylons' prisoner anywhere. He had acted unlawfully.

"Tell the Lord Sark that my only aim is to find the pirates who stole his planet's crystals. To do that, I need the prisoner's assistance."

These words seemed to relax Sark a little. Next time he spoke, his voice had lost some of its sharpness. But still he was not entirely happy. Amy Adair was his captive, he said. She had committed a crime against the Greylon nation and he was reluctant to let her go.

"You are not letting her go," Kit replied,

eyeing the alien leader with unyielding determination. "You are putting her in the hands of Star Quest. We need her to catch those pirates."

At last, Sark seemed content. His eagle-like head nodded as he gave his consent and there was a hint of a smile in his eyes.

"But remember," he warned, "we shall be watching. Whatever you do, we shall be watching…"

A DIFFICULT DECISION

Kit was as relieved to be back on the *Icarus 2* as the rest of the crew were to see him: the Greylons had made him feel very uneasy. What's more, he had observed, through his cybereye, there were definite signs that the Greylons were preparing their fleet for war. Time was running out and he had to find those pirates fast.

Kit introduced Amy to the others and quickly told them her story and of her offer to help. Red alone seemed unconvinced.

What if she really were one of the pirates, he said suspiciously. She could lead them straight into a trap.

"Amy is not a pirate," Kit snapped. "Nor is she a prisoner. Until we get back to Earth she is our guest and will be treated like one. Is that clear? Red?"

Red huffed and scowled. "You're the captain," he mumbled.

"That's right, I am," Kit said. Then he turned to Amy.

"You know these pirates, Amy," he said. "Where do you think they are now?"

Amy frowned. "There's a deserted spacestation at the edge of the Greylon Galaxy, where the pirates have their base," she said. "They go there to put fuel in their ship and to hide sometimes, when they're being chased. They could be there now." She pursed her lips and shook her head. "But I couldn't say for sure. It's hard to tell with Silver."

"Silver's their leader," Kit explained. Then he, too, frowned. "I think we'd better speak to the Commander. Can you link us up, Josie?"

"You bet yer, skipper," Josie replied perkily.

She swivelled her chair to face her console, then flicked a couple of switches. A red light flared up on her control board. She pushed a couple of buttons, tapped something in on her keyboard and listened carefully for an instant, putting one hand up to her headphones. Another red light went on. She turned to face the others and shrugged. Her expression was unusually serious.

"There's a malfunction," she said. "Some kind of interference. I can't contact Earth."

"Oh, that's all we need," Red grumbled. "What are we supposed to do now?"

Kit sat down heavily in his chair. "Sunny, I-See, you're the brainy ones. What do you suggest?"

Sunny's eyes blinked in thought, the creamy half-moon on his forehead creasing with concentration. "We could send out scanner waves," he proposed. "Try and find them that way. But it might take time."

"Mmm," said Kit – "and time is one thing we don't have. I-See?"

I-See's antenna quivered a little as he started to speak. "I believe the opinion of Doctor Patel to be correct," he said. "The scanner waves are most likely to locate the pirates."

"Mmm," said Kit. He frowned as he considered the alternatives, each of which seemed to be a risk. Either they set out at once for the pirate base and risked going on a wild goose chase, or they waited for the scanner waves to find their target and risked running out of time…

Kit nodded his head and grimaced. "Right," he said with sudden decisiveness, "we go for the spacestation. Josie, Amy, I want its exact location. Red, prepare to get this ship moving. Sunny, I'm going to need maximum power."

For the next few minutes the ship bustled with activity as the crew carried out their various tasks. Amy joined Josie at her computer terminal. They scanned a space map of the Greylon Galaxy to find the abandoned spacestation where the pirates had their base. When Amy had identified it, Josie called out the co-ordinates to Red.

"5-7-0, 9-X-Z!" she cried.

"Roger," said Red and he tapped in the

numbers on his navigation board. Now the controls were locked into the right flight path. An instant later, they were speeding through space.

"How long before we get there, Red?" Kit asked.

"About forty starminutes, Captain," Red replied.

Kit pulled a face. Forty starminutes was too long. "We need a bit more speed, Sunny," he said. "Can you push the engines any harder?"

"If I do, we will be in danger of burning up too much fuel," Sunny said. "We may not have enough to get back to Earth."

"There may not be an Earth to go back to if we don't catch these pirates," Kit said darkly. "I want full power."

"OK, Captain," Sunny said. "Full power it is." He pulled down two levers as far as they would go. The ship shuddered for a second and there was a roar from the engines. Now they were really flying.

As the ship whirled through the blackness, Kit sat tensely in his chair, staring at the control screen, hoping that his decision had been the right one. If it wasn't, well, the outcome was too awful to consider. He just had to be right.

The next half-hour was the longest of Kit's life. It seemed like they'd never arrive at the pirates' base. At last, though, Red announced that the spacestation was in scanner-sight and an instant later it appeared on the screen. It looked ordinary enough.

"Run a check on it, Josie," he ordered. "I want to know if there are any life forms there."

"OK, skip," Josie replied. Kit waited impatiently while his sister tapped in various commands into her computer console and studied the results.

"Well?" he demanded.

"Nothing," Josie said heavily. "The spacestation is still deserted."

Kit's spirits sank. This was just what he

hadn't wanted to hear. The pirates weren't at their base, which meant they could be anywhere. They could be in another galaxy by now. There was a collective sigh of disappointment. Even I-See was affected by the general mood of gloom: his monitor went black.

"I told you not to trust her," Red said bitterly, nodding at Amy.

"This *is* the place," said Amy fiercely, but, beneath her defiance, she seemed close to tears.

"We believe you, Amy," Kit said quietly. "It's not your fault. No one's to blame."

The ship hung silently in space, surrounded by blackness, the empty spacestation tantalizingly close – and yet, it seemed, of no help whatsoever. Staring at the control screen, Kit was becalmed like his ship, and brooding. What should they do now? Was there anything they *could* do? Beside him, suddenly, Red squirmed in his chair, fingers punching, shouting, "Ship approaching! Ninety galactic metres to starboard! Appearing on screen now."

Kit's eyes flicked into life as he focused on the screen … and there it was, zipping towards them out of the darkness, skull and crossbones clearly visible on its bow: the pirate ship! And its laser guns were already flashing!

SILVER!

···

"Defence shields up! Battle stations, everyone!" Kit screamed.

Quick as a flash, Red spun the *Icarus 2* into evasive orbit, but already the small Questship was reeling from the impact of the first burst of laser fire. All five crew members rocked in their seats. Amy Adair, the only one who wasn't strapped in, was hurled across the control room. She landed in a heap at I-See's feet.

"Are you OK?" Kit hissed anxiously.

"Yeah, just about," Amy said, wincing. "I think I've hurt my ankle."

"I-See, strap Amy into a seat," Kit ordered. "Then get back into position. We're going to need all hands to escape from this." He spun round in his chair.

"What's the damage, Sunny?" he asked.

"Not too disastrous, Captain," Sunny replied. "The main body's all right. But the starboard engine is not functioning properly."

It amazed Kit how cool Sunny remained even in the hottest of situations. "Can you repair it?" he asked urgently.

"Eventually," Sunny replied matter-of-factly. "Not immediately."

"Oh, great," Kit said with a deep sigh.

"Pirate ship coming in on the port side!" Red cried.

Kit stared at the control screen. He knew he had to think and act fast. It was all very well practising what to do in class at the Academy, but this was the real thing. This was the moment he had to prove himself a real Star Quest Captain.

"OK, Red, hold it steady," he said.

"But, Kit, the pirates are going to attack!" Red said incredulously, panic rising in his voice.

"I know, Red," Kit said. "I want you to hold your course until the instant they fire.

Then move like lightning."

"I hope you know what you're doing, skip," said Josie.

"When they use their weapons, they're using up a lot of power," said Kit. "Isn't that right, Sunny?"

"Perfectly correct," Sunny nodded.

"And with one engine down, we need them to use up as much power as possible," Kit continued. "So, hold it steady, Red. Josie, have you locked on to them? I need to know the second those lasers fire."

"OK, skip," Josie called.

Kit turned to his navigator. "Then it's up to you, Red," he said. The two boys faced each other, eye to eye for a moment, then Red nodded. The panic had passed now. His look was full of determination.

The pirate ship drew closer on an exact collision course.

"They think they've crippled us," Kit said excitedly.

"Stand by, everyone, they're moving in for

the kill." The Star Quest crew sat tensely in their seats, all poised over their controls, waiting for the call to action.

"I hope you're as fast as Colonel Alexander said," Kit murmured under his breath to the ship. There was sweat on his brow and in his palms. This manoeuvre was extremely risky: if they were a split-second late in evading, they'd all be blown to pieces...

"Now!" shrieked Josie suddenly as the pirate ship opened fire again and Red sent the *Icarus 2* spinning out of its path.

The manoeuvre worked. A quick check revealed that the laser attack had scorched the Questship's belly, but no structural damage had been done.

"Now, turn about!" Kit ordered. "We're going to engage!"

Even with its damaged engine, the small ship was able to change direction with amazing speed. The larger ship had no time to alter its course before it found the *Icarus 2* on its tail, lasers at the ready.

"Try to open a communications link, Josie," Kit commanded, his eyes fixed on the control screen.

"OK, skip," Josie answered.

This time, she was successful. As Kit stared, a face appeared on the control screen: a scarred, hairy, snarling face, with a patch over one eye.

"Mr Silver, I presume," Kit said.

The expression on the face became a mocking grin. "Aye, I'm Silver," he said. "And who are you? The Space Kid?"

"I'm Captain Kit Johnson of the Questship *Icarus 2* and I order you to surrender," said Kit icily.

Silver frowned. He looked almost puzzled. "Captain Johnson of the *Icarus 2* you say?" he inquired.

"Yes, Mr Silver. I believe you know my father, Captain Marcus Johnson of the Questship *Icarus*."

Silver's face glowered with hostility. "I know Captain Marcus Johnson all right," he spat venomously. "So you're his pup, eh?"

"I'm a Star Quest Captain and I order you to surrender," Kit repeated.

This time Silver laughed. "Do you hear that, lads?" he said to his fellow pirates. "The boy orders me to surrender." He faced Kit again with a snarl. "You're the one to surrender," he said. "It's your ship that's been hit, laddy, not mine."

Kit stared into the control screen with a look of steel. "If you don't surrender," he said, "I shall be forced to open fire."

"Then fire," hissed Silver and the screen went dark.

"Communication link's broken," said Josie.

"They're on the move!" called Red.

"OK, I-See," Kit said, "this is your moment. I want them stopped but not destroyed."

"Understood, Captain," I-See burbled, his monitor bursting into life with images of explosions. "Lasers now activating."

I-See's aim was perfect. A split-second

later, a line of laser fire hit the pirate ship on its port side. Then another line found its target on the starboard side. A third line blasted the tail. The pirate ship juddered one way, then the other. It flipped about like a fish out of water, then came to a complete halt. The control screen lit up again and Silver's angry face appeared.

"Curse you, boy," he said. "You've killed my ship."

"I gave you fair warning," Kit replied. "I told you to surrender."

Silver continued to glower at Kit for a few moments, as if trying to stare him out. Then his face took on a twisted, mocking leer. "I'll never surrender to you, boy," he declared.

Kit was puzzled by Silver's words and his sudden change of expression. He had to surrender, there was no way he could escape. Yet he was smiling. Was he mad?

"Don't trust him, Kit!" Amy shrieked.

"They've got another weapon!" Josie gasped, peering at the scanner monitor before her. "Beneath their ship and it's pointing straight at us!"

Now, with a horrible feeling of doom, Kit understood. Silver had outsmarted him. He still had one card up his sleeve: a deadly card, against which Kit was helpless. All he could do was spin away again and hope for the best. But this time, the enemy would be ready for his move and the chance of evasion was slim.

"Prepare to spin, Red," he said softly to his navigator, without taking his gaze from the screen. He watched Silver's eyes, seeking the sign that would give the order to fire. He could feel sweat trickling down his spine as he waited, waited…

"Go!" he shrieked at last as Silver's eyes widened in crazy triumph.

There was a blinding flash of white light. The *Icarus* spun away – but too slowly. There was no escape. It was all over.

This, Kit knew, was the end.

A SOMBRE RETURN

He couldn't believe it. He was alive. Somehow, incredibly, the *Icarus 2* was still in one piece and he was still alive. Kit touched his body, his head, then looked about him, amazed. Everyone was still there, the ship was flying. His eyes lifted to the control screen: all was black, except for a small ball of fire that dropped away into space like a meteor and then vanished before his eyes. There was no sign of the pirate ship.

Kit stared into the blank control screen, too dazed to speak. Around him, the rest of the crew were in the grip of the same eerie, shocked silence. It didn't last long. A moment later a high-pitched receiving call sounded and a familiar face filled the screen – grey, eagle-like, beady-eyed.

"Sark!" Kit exclaimed, snapping into life.

The Greylon Lord nodded and spoke.

"Lord Sark thanks us for leading him to the crystal thieves," I-See translated as the Greylon Lord's message flashed up on his body monitor. "He says our mission is now over and that we can return to Earth. There will be no war between our two galaxies. He wishes us a safe journey."

Kit listened with growing anger as he understood what had happened: Sark had used the *Icarus* as bait to find the pirates. Then he'd acted with ruthless and deadly power.

"Tell the Lord Sark," he said fiercely, "that he should not have destroyed the pirate ship. It was not right."

"Hey, steady, Kit," said Red nervously. "He saved our lives."

"He could have disabled the pirate ship at any time," Kit insisted. "He didn't need to destroy it. That was murder."

Sark stiffened as he heard Kit's message. Then he growled out a message of his own.

"Lord Sark says you have much to learn of

the ways of space, Captain," I-See translated. "He orders us to leave his galaxy at once."

Kit glared at the screen, smouldering. Sark had played with their lives as though they were mere toys. Kit was furious, but there was nothing now that he could do.

"Very well," he said, finally. "Red, plot a course for Earth. We're going home."

"Not a moment too soon either," Red remarked. He had no wish to stay an instant longer in this place. He didn't like the look of the Greylon Lord at all.

The mood on the journey home was one of quiet concentration. The mission had been successful, but no one really felt like celebrating. They all knew that Sark had tricked them and they didn't like it. Kit was especially quiet. To be a real Star Quest Captain he would have to learn to think more clearly, to be tougher and more wary. Both Silver and Sark had outwitted him and the *Icarus* was fortunate to have escaped intact and with all its crew alive and well. In another situation things could have been very different...

Kit's ambition of being a Star Quest Adventurer like his dad seemed a long, long way off. Dr Marcus Johnson would never have been caught out the way he had been, Kit was sure of that. Thinking of his dad, Kit was suddenly overcome by a feeling of disappointment that the journey had brought him no nearer to discovering what had happened to him. If only he'd had a chance to question Silver, the mystery might now have been solved. When Sark had destroyed the pirate ship, he'd destroyed Kit's hopes of finding out about his father too. Well, for the moment anyway.

While Kit sat deep in thought, Josie ran a computer check on Amy's story and her home, Spartacus 9. Kit believed what Amy had told him, but he knew that the Commander would not be so easily convinced: he would expect proper proof. So Kit had ordered the check. As it was going on, the two girls exchanged stories about their lives and their families. Josie told Amy about her father's disappearance.

"You must miss *your* father too," said Josie. "And your mother."

Amy shook her head and her large green eyes filled with sadness. "They were both killed when the pirates raided our colony. I have no family now."

"I'm sorry," Josie said gently. She put her arm on the older girl's shoulder.

"We're through Middle Space!" Red announced gleefully. "We are now entering our own galaxy." At this news, even Sunny's usually impassive face broke into a broad smile. On I-See's body monitor a satellite picture of Earth appeared with the words "Home, sweet home" underneath. Kit turned in his skipper's seat and smiled at Amy.

"Welcome back to Earth," he said warmly.

A JOB WELL DONE

....

"You have done well, Captain Kit Johnson."
The Commander nodded his appreciation as
he spoke. His lined face looked a lot more
relaxed than last time Kit was in his office.
"I would call that a very successful first
mission."

"Thank you, sir," Kit replied. He still
wasn't as content as the Commander
appeared to be, but he didn't feel it was his
place to say so. "We did our best."

"And your best was excellent." Now
Colonel Alexander joined in the praise.

"I had an excellent crew, sir," Kit said
simply, but he was pleased and honoured by
the Colonel's approval. It wasn't every day
you were praised by a space hero with a Gold
Lightning Flash.

"Indeed," the Commander agreed. He put

his palms together and stared thoughtfully at Kit. "I understand from your report that the *Icarus* sustained some damage in your fight with the pirates."

"One of the engines was damaged, sir," Kit said. "And we had some communications problems. We couldn't contact you here on Earth."

"Well, that just makes your achievement all the greater," the Commander commented. "A Star Quest Captain must be able to think for himself. And you proved that you can do that."

"Thank you, sir," Kit said, his face glowing with pride. He couldn't have asked for a better welcome.

But the Commander was not entirely happy. "I must point out to you, however," he continued, "that a Star Quest Captain must never allow his heart to rule his head." He looked at Kit sternly. "You should not have offended the Greylon Lord. You were in his galaxy, bound by his laws. In offending him you could have ruined the whole mission." Kit swallowed hard. The Commander's words stung him sharply.

"With respect, sir," he said, "the Academy teaches us to destroy only as a last defence. Lord Sark was in no danger, yet he deliberately destroyed the pirate ship and killed all those on board…"

"In his galaxy, Captain, he may do as he pleases," the Commander insisted. "Star Quest has no right to tell him what to do. Is that understood?" His grey eyes were like slate as they confronted Kit's own.

Kit looked down. "Yes, sir," he said meekly.

"Good," said the Commander. Then his gaze softened. "Because the Colonel and I wouldn't want to lose our newest and brightest Star Quest Captain after just a couple of missions…" He glanced across at Colonel Alexander with raised eyebrows and the Colonel nodded back.

Something in the tone of the Commander's voice made Kit look up sharply.

"A couple of missions," he repeated. "You mean…"

"I mean that I have decided to keep the *Icarus 2* as a Questship," the Commander stated. "One of our older vessels will take over its training function. The *Icarus 2* will be used for special missions – a kind of troubleshooting ship if you like. You, Kit, and your crew will continue at the Academy, but must be prepared at any time to be called into action. You will report to Colonel Alexander."

"Yes, sir, thank you, sir," said Kit, pride once again swelling within him. This was what he had dreamed of all through his childhood. He couldn't wait to tell his mother and Josie – and the others too.

"Good. That's settled," said the Commander. He smiled broadly now. "There's just one more thing. We have a new recruit to the Academy and I would like you to take her under your wing and help her settle in. You know each other already." He pushed a button on his desk and the door slid aside. "Enter, please, Cadet Adair."

"Amy!" Kit cried. This he really hadn't expected. "They've taken you on."

"Well, after the glowing report you gave us," said Colonel Alexander, "how could we possibly refuse?"

Kit beamed at his new friend and Amy grinned back. She looked quite different from when Kit had last seen her; now she was dressed smartly in a Star Quest uniform, though she still wore the gold bracelets on her arms.

"Right," said the Commander. "That really is all. You are both dismissed."

Later Kit sat with Amy and Josie in the Star Quest Academy's leisure lounge. Sunny and I-See were there, too, playing a game of chess on the computeroid's body monitor. Kit told the two girls about his meeting with the Commander and Colonel Alexander.

"Well, still, I think you were right," said Josie. "What Sark did was, well, inhuman."

"I agree," said Amy.

"Me too," said another familiar voice. The three Academy pupils glanced up to see the burly figure of the *Icarus*'s navigator standing over them. They'd been too wrapped up in their talk to notice him walk in. His pale freckly face looked down at them seriously.

"What you said was right, Kit," Red said. "I didn't think so at the time, but, well, now I do." There was a brief, awkward pause before he continued. "You did a very good job."

The corners of his mouth turned up in a shy sort of smile. "I couldn't have done better," he added.

Kit smiled back at his second-in-command. "You did a great job, too," he said. Then he raised his palm to his heart, his fingers touching the Star Quest emblem in a gesture of respect and friendship. Red returned the gesture. Then he turned and walked away.

"He's not so bad," Josie said.

"He's an excellent navigator, that's for sure," Kit declared with deep admiration. He looked across at his sister. "You were good out there too, sis," he said affectionately. "Dad would have been proud of you."

"He'd have been proud of both of us," Josie agreed.

Kit nodded and stared out into the night sky. "One day, Dad," he whispered, his words little more than air. "I'll find you, one day…"